THIS BOOK BELONGS TO

Amihan

With God's Richest
blessing

Grandpadidi & Gammy

GIVEN BY

Aug 2007

DATE

A
Treasury
of Bible
Promises

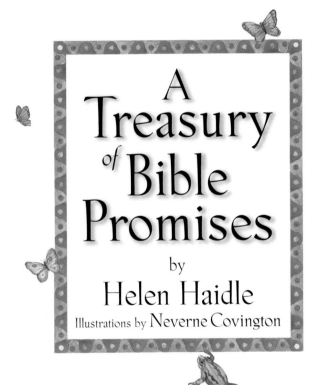

A Treasury of Bible Promises

by

Helen Haidle

Illustrations by Neverne Covington

Zonderkidz

A Treasury of Bible Promises
Copyright 2002 by Helen Haidle
Illustrations copyright © 2002 by Neverne Covington

Zonder**kidz**.™

The children's group of Zondervan

Grand Rapids, Michigan 49530
www.zonderkidz.com

ISBN 0–310–70032–9

Editor: Gwen Ellis
Art Direction and Design: Lisa Workman
Printed in China

02 03 04 06 07 /❖ HC/ 10 9 8 7 6 5 4 3 2 1

To Karen Anderson

I praise God for your faith and your friendship
And for *all* the many ways you have blessed me.

Contents

The Greatest Treasure
in the World

If you were looking for the world's greatest treasure, where would you look? Would you:

- Dive deep in the sea in search of sunken ships?
- Sail to a faraway island and dig for a buried treasure chest?
- Sail around the world in a hot air balloon looking down below for gold mines?

God put the world's greatest treasure in a place where every one of us can discover it. It is found in the pages of a book—the Bible, God's Word. When you dig into God's Word, you will find . . .

God's Promises!

His promises are worth more than gold, jewels, riches, or any other treasure in the world!

Treasure Nuggets from God's Word

"The LORD kept all of the good promises he had made to the people of Israel. Everyone of them came true."

Joshua 21:45

"The law you gave is worth more to me than thousands of pieces of silver and gold … Your words are very sweet to my taste! They are sweeter than honey to me."

Psalm 119:72, 103

"I'm filled with joy because of God's promise.
It's like finding a great fortune [treasure]."

Psalm 119:162

"What our God says will stand forever."

Isaiah 40:8

"Every word of God is perfect."

Proverbs 30:5 (NLT)

2

God Is the Promise Maker

God is the only one who never breaks a promise.

God is the great Promise Maker—and Promise Keeper.

- Because God is all-powerful and almighty, he is strong enough to do what he promises.
- When God says something is going to happen, it *will!*

God can do anything!

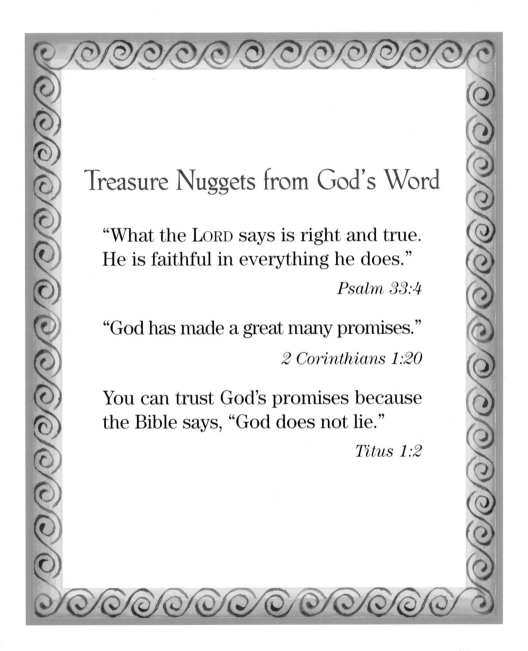

Treasure Nuggets from God's Word

"What the LORD says is right and true. He is faithful in everything he does."

Psalm 33:4

"God has made a great many promises."

2 Corinthians 1:20

You can trust God's promises because the Bible says, "God does not lie."

Titus 1:2

3

God Keeps His Promises

Read this story in Genesis 6:9–9:17.

Long ago Noah trusted God and did what was right. But everyone else on earth did not trust God.

God decided to send a flood to destroy everything on earth.

God told Noah to build a big boat called an ark. God promised to keep Noah and his family safe inside the ark.

Noah trusted God, so he started building the huge boat. Many people came to see what Noah was doing. They laughed at him. They didn't believe God would send a flood.

But Noah kept right on building. He knew God would keep his promise.

When the ark was finished, God sent pairs of animals and pairs of birds to the ark so they would be safe from the flood that was coming.

Noah, his wife, his three sons, and his sons' wives went into the ark with all the animals. And then it began to rain—just as God said it would.

It rained for forty days and forty nights before it finally stopped. There was so much water covering the earth that it took five months for the water to go down.

At last the ark came to rest on top of a mountain. Everyone inside the boat was safe—just as God had promised.

Then God told Noah, "Come out of the ark. Bring your wife, and your sons and their wives. Bring every creature that is with you."

So Noah came out. He built an altar and he thanked God for keeping every promise.

God also gave Noah one more promise. It was for everyone who would ever live on earth.

Treasure Nuggets from God's Word

"A flood will never destroy the earth again . . .
I have put my rainbow in the clouds."

Genesis 9:11, 13

"I have put my rainbow in the clouds. It will
be a sign of the covenant between me and
the earth . . . I will remember that my
covenant will last forever."

Genesis 9:13, 16

"The One who promised is faithful."

Hebrews 10:23

God's Amazing Rainbow

- A rainbow forms when sunlight hits millions of raindrops.
- The light bends and separates into seven colors—red, orange, yellow, green, blue, indigo, and violet.
- Red light bends the least. It always appears on top of the rainbow.
- Violet light bends the most, and it always appears on the bottom of the rainbow.

Make Your Own Promise Rainbow

- You will need paper and colored pens or pencils.
- On the paper draw a picture of a rainbow with all its colors.
- Tape your rainbow on a window.
- Whenever you look out the window, let the rainbow remind you of God's promise to Noah and to the animals.

4

God Loves You

Doesn't it feel good to know someone loves you?

But do you know that love is more than a feeling? Love does something for others.

Love

- Gives to others.
- Takes care of someone.
- Does all it can to help others be happy.

Where does this kind of love come from?

The Bible says that all love comes from God.

"Let us love one another, because love comes from God ... "God is love."

1 John 4:7, 8

"What is love? It is not that we loved God. It is that he loved us and sent his Son."

1 John 4:10

How Big Is God's Love?

What is the biggest thing you have ever seen? Is it

- a mountain?
- a tall skyscraper?
- a big ship?
- a huge whale?

God's love for us is bigger than anything we can find on earth.

God's love is as big as the sky!

The great big sky above the earth is the highest thing anyone can see. And guess what? God's love for us is even higher than that!

"God's love for those who have respect for him is as high as the heavens are above the earth."

Psalm 103:11

How Many Stars Are in the Sky?

- You can see 2,500 to 6,000 stars without a telescope.
- Many more stars cannot be seen—even with a telescope. God filled the sky with over 100 trillion billion stars! No one except God could ever count them all.
- The Bible says that God not only counts the stars, he gives each one a name.

How Far Is the Moon?

The moon is the heavenly body nearest to the earth. But it is still about 225,000 miles away. That is as far as driving around the earth about nine times!

The moon looks close to us. But if you traveled one hundred miles an hour, it would take you three months to reach the moon even if you drove every hour of every day.

Look Up!

Take a blanket outside on the next starry night. Lie down and look up at the sky. Even the closest stars you can see are very far away. When you look at the sky above, remember that God's love is bigger than everything you can see. And remember that God knows all the stars names and he knows your name, too. Isn't that wonderful to know?

Treasure Nuggets from God's Word

"LORD, your love is as high as the heavens. Your faithful love reaches up to the skies."

Psalm 36:5

"God is loving toward everything he has made."

Psalm 145:13

The LORD said, "I have loved you with a love that lasts forever."

Jeremiah 31:3

"Nothing at all can ever separate us from God's love."

Romans 8:39

5

God Holds You Close

Sometimes it's important to hold some-one's hand and stick close to that person so you don't get lost.

- Do you ever hold someone's hand tightly when you're afraid?
- Do your parents ever hold on to you in a crowd to keep you close?
- Do you like to be hugged when you've had a scary nightmare?

God promises to hold on to you and never let you go. The Bible says he holds you by your hand. God loves you and doesn't want you to be afraid.

"I am the LORD your God. I take hold of your right hand. I say to you, 'Do not be afraid. I will help you.'"

Isaiah 41:13

Jesus also promised to hold us in his powerful hands. How strong do you think his hands are?

Jesus said, "No one can steal my sheep out of my hand."

John 10:28

His love is so strong that no one in the world could ever pull us from his grip!

Jesus said, "I am the Mighty One."

Revelation 1:8

Wherever we go, God's hand will hold us.

"LORD, suppose I were to rise with the sun in the east and then cross over to the west where it sinks into the ocean. Your hand would always be there to guide me. Your right hand would still be holding me close."

Psalm 139:9–10

Be Still and Know

The LORD says, "Be still, and know that I am God."

Psalm 46:10

When you're afraid:

- Sit and breathe deeply.
- Pretend you're putting all your fears into your cupped hands.
- Lift your hands and give your troubles to God.
- Say to yourself, "Everything's all right. My worries are in God's hands."

Treasure Nuggets from God's Word

"LORD ... your strong right hand keeps me going."

Psalm 18:35

"I trust in you, LORD ... My whole life is in your hands."

Psalm 31:14–15

"The LORD's powerful right hand has done mighty things!"

Psalm 118:16

"Put yourselves under God's mighty hand."

1 Peter 5:6

God Takes Care of You

God knows all about you. He knows what you need and what will make you happy. Most of all, you can be sure:

"God's powerful right hand will take good care of you."

Isaiah 41:10

Why Worry?

Just about everyone worries sometimes.

- What are some things you worry about?
- Can we change anything by worrying?
- Will our worrying change other people?
- Does it do any good to worry?

It's God's job to take care of us. That means our job is to *stop worrying* and *start trusting* God!

Jesus doesn't want us to worry, either. He wants us to trust God. He said, "I tell you, do not worry."

Matthew 6:25

Jesus said worrying doesn't do much. He said, "Can you add even one hour to your life by worrying? You can't do that very little thing. So why worry about the rest?"

Luke 12:25–26

Look At the Wild Flowers

Jesus said, "See how the wild flowers grow. They don't work or make clothing. But . . . not even Solomon in all of his glory was dressed like one of those flowers.

"If that is how God dresses the wild grass, won't he dress you even better?

"So don't worry."

Matthew 6:28–31

Jesus said, "Don't say, 'What will we eat?' Or, 'What will we drink?' Or, 'What will we wear?' People who are ungodly run after all of those things. Your Father who is in heaven knows that you need them.

But put God's kingdom first. Do what he wants you to do. Then all of those things will also be given to you."

Matthew 6:31–33

Jesus always took care of people. Once he used a boy's lunch to feed a hungry crowd. It was just five small loaves of bread and two small fish. But that lunch fed more than five thousand people!

Even when it seems impossible, we need to trust God. He can do the impossible! God will take care of everything.

Activity Page

- Cut pictures of flowers from magazines and paste them on a sheet of paper.
- Write these words on your paper:

  "Don't worry!
  God cares for every flower.
  God cares for you."

- You can keep your picture yourself or give it to a friend as a reminder not to worry.

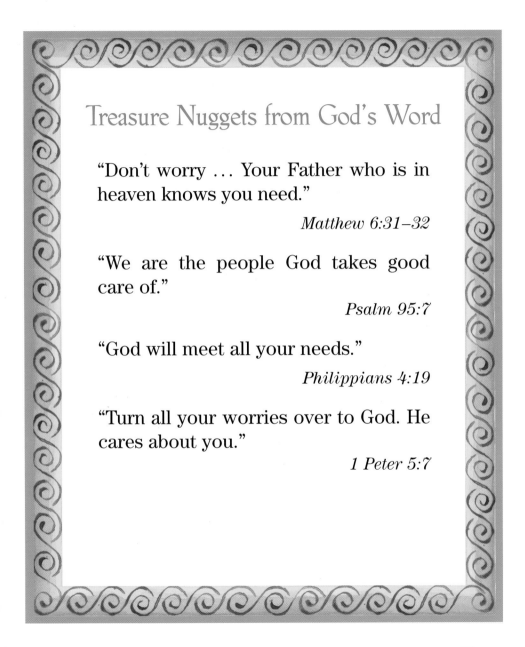

Treasure Nuggets from God's Word

"Don't worry ... Your Father who is in heaven knows you need."

Matthew 6:31–32

"We are the people God takes good care of."

Psalm 95:7

"God will meet all your needs."

Philippians 4:19

"Turn all your worries over to God. He cares about you."

1 Peter 5:7

7

God Saves You

Think about this:

- Nobody in the world lives a perfect life.
- Nobody loves God enough.
- Nobody loves other people enough.
- All people are mean to others at times.
- Everyone has times when he or she feels selfish or angry.
- Every person has a big problem— that problem is sin.

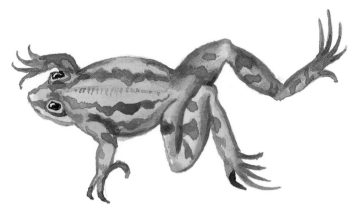

We sin when we

- Break God's laws.
- Love ourselves more than we love God.
- Don't do what we know we should do.
- Don't put God first in our lives.

But there is hope for all of us:

"While we were still sinners, Christ died for us."

Romans 5:8

Who Has Sinned?

Everyone has sinned. No one measures up to God's glory."

Romans 3:23

"No one is right with God, no one at all. No one understands. No one trusts in God. All of them have turned away."

Romans 3:10–12

When we do wrong at home, our parents are going to punish us. When we do wrong in God's eyes, we are going to have to be punished. So since all of us have done wrong, we all deserve to be punished.

Help!
What are we going to do
about this problem?

God knew we couldn't fix our problem by ourselves. So he made a way for us to be saved from our sin. Here's how:

God sent an angel to tell Joseph, "Mary is going to have a son. You must give him the name Jesus. That is because he will save his people from their sins."

Matthew 1:21

God sent his own dear Son to be our Savior. That's great! But what is a Savior? What does a Savior do?

- A Savior rescues us.
- A Savior suffers the punishment we deserve.
- A Savior forgives us.
- A Savior makes us right with God.

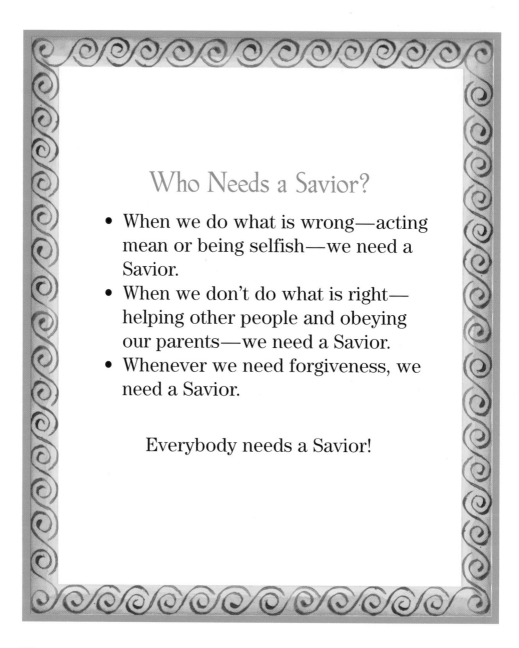

Who Needs a Savior?

- When we do what is wrong—acting mean or being selfish—we need a Savior.
- When we don't do what is right—helping other people and obeying our parents—we need a Savior.
- Whenever we need forgiveness, we need a Savior.

Everybody needs a Savior!

That's why Jesus gave his life on the cross—so we could be saved, forgiven, and made right with God. Jesus didn't die for us because we deserved it or were good enough. He died for us because we didn't deserve it and we were not right with God.

Is Jesus *Your* Savior?

You can ask Jesus to be your Savior now. Just pray,

> "Dear Jesus, thank you for loving me.
> Thank you for giving your life for me.
> Thank you for taking my punishment.
> Please forgive all I've done wrong.
> Come into my heart. Be my Savior.
> Help me live a new life with you."

Now Jesus is *your* Savior!

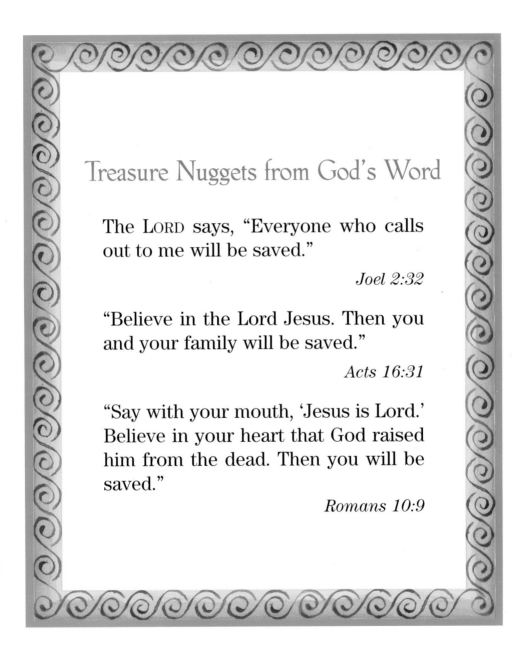

Treasure Nuggets from God's Word

The LORD says, "Everyone who calls out to me will be saved."

Joel 2:32

"Believe in the Lord Jesus. Then you and your family will be saved."

Acts 16:31

"Say with your mouth, 'Jesus is Lord.' Believe in your heart that God raised him from the dead. Then you will be saved."

Romans 10:9

8

God Forgives You

God wants us to love him most of all, then love others and do what's right. But when we *don't*, we must remember:

- God wants to forgive us.
- We can ask God for forgiveness anytime we need to.
- We can be sure that God will forgive us when we ask!

"The blood of Jesus, God's Son, makes us pure from all sin."

1 John 1:7

When we ask God to forgive us through his Son, Jesus, he will make us pure. God will make our whole life new and clean in his sight. Then he will look at us as if we had never sinned. Isn't that amazing?

White As Snow

God says, "Even though your sins are bright red, they will be as white as snow ... But you have to be willing to change and obey me."

Isaiah 1:18–19

It is hard to find anything as white as new snow. But there is one thing as white and clean as snow—forgiven sins.

When King David knew he had sinned, he was willing to change and obey God. So he prayed and asked God to forgive him. Then he wrote,

"Blessed is the man whose sin the LORD never counts against him."

Psalm 32:2

"God has removed our lawless acts from us as far as the east is from the west."

Psalm 103:12

What Happens When God Forgives?

- All the bad things we've done are removed from our lives.
- Our lives are wiped clean.
- God throws everything bad into the deepest sea.
- God will never remember any of our sins.

Does God Forget?

When God forgives something, he will *never* bring it up again! Your sins are gone forever.

Isn't that wonderful? Let's be thankful to God.

"LORD, who is a God like you?... You forgive your people when they do what is wrong ... You will throw all of our sins into the bottom of the sea."

Micah 7:18–19

Time to Forgive

Jesus said, "Forgive people when they sin against you. If you do, your Father who is in heaven will also forgive you."

Matthew 6:14

- If you need God's forgiveness, just ask him.
- If you're holding grudges, ask God to help you forgive.
- If you've hurt someone, ask that person for forgiveness.

Treasure Nuggets from God's Word

God says, "I will not remember your sins anymore."

Isaiah 43:25

"If we admit that we have sinned, God will forgive us our sins. He will forgive every wrong thing we have done. He will make us pure."

1 John 1:9

"Jesus gave his life to pay for our sins."

1 John 2:2

God Hears Your Prayer

Prayer is a heart-to-heart talk with God. And God is always listening. So we can

- Tell God how we feel.
- Tell God what we need.
- Talk to him about everything in our lives.

It doesn't matter how we pray, where we are, or what we're doing. God always hears us when we pray.

Here's a great promise for everyone who prays—even kids.

"Ask, and it will be given to you. Search, and you will find. Knock, and the door will be opened to you. Everyone who asks will receive."

Matthew 7:7–8

Pray Alone

Being alone helps us think about what we're saying to God.

- Pray when you're alone.
- Pray in a special place—like beside your bed.

Jesus said, "When you pray, go into your room. Close the door and pray to your Father, who can't be seen. He will reward you. Your Father sees what is done secretly."

Matthew 6:6

Pray with Others

Here's a great promise for people who pray together:

Jesus said, "Suppose two of you on earth agree about anything you ask for. My Father in heaven will do it for you."

Matthew 18:19

Wow! Isn't that a neat promise?

Keep on Praying

Read this story in 1 Kings 18:16–46.

Long ago Elijah held a prayer contest. Some prophets prayed all day, asking their god, Baal, to send fire to prove he was the strongest god. Baal never answered.

Then Elijah asked God to send fire to prove he was the true God.

Immediately, fire fell from heaven! All the people cried, "The LORD is the one and only God!"

Then Elijah climbed to the top of the mountain. He prayed that God would send rain. It hadn't rained for three years!

Elijah asked his servant to look toward the sea. The servant saw nothing. So Elijah kept praying.

When Elijah prayed the *seventh* time, his servant said, "I see a cloud!"

Then Elijah knew God had heard his prayers! Soon there was a downpour of rain!

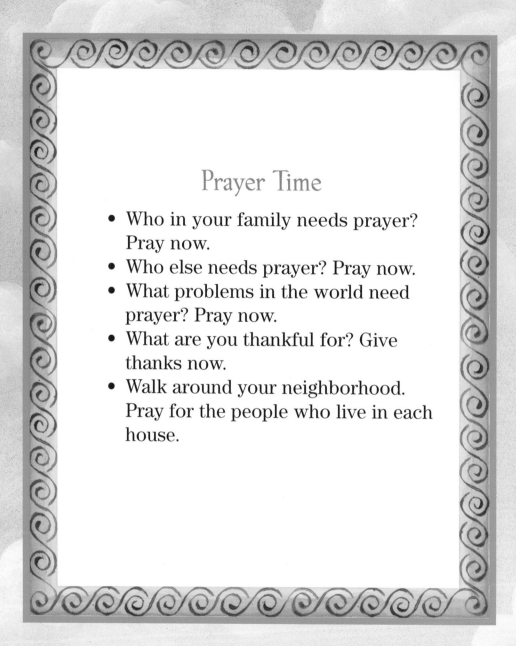

Prayer Time

- Who in your family needs prayer? Pray now.
- Who else needs prayer? Pray now.
- What problems in the world need prayer? Pray now.
- What are you thankful for? Give thanks now.
- Walk around your neighborhood. Pray for the people who live in each house.

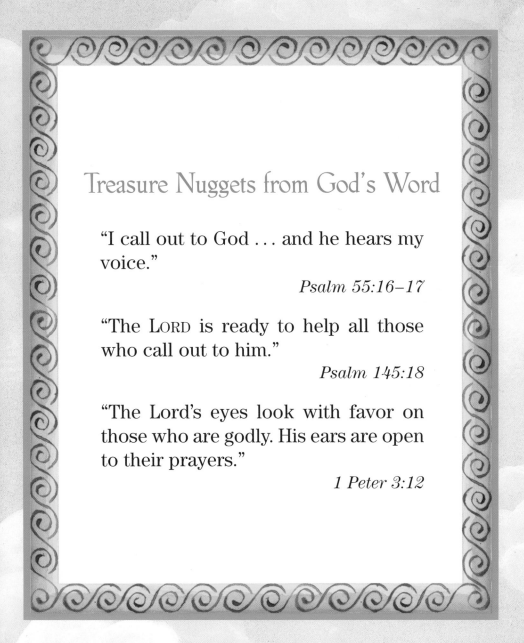

Treasure Nuggets from God's Word

"I call out to God . . . and he hears my voice."

Psalm 55:16–17

"The LORD is ready to help all those who call out to him."

Psalm 145:18

"The Lord's eyes look with favor on those who are godly. His ears are open to their prayers."

1 Peter 3:12

10

God Answers Your Prayer

God is ready and waiting to give good gifts to those who ask. When you pray, you can always trust God to answer.

"The LORD is my name. Call out to me. I will answer you."

Jeremiah 33:2–3

Jesus said, "Suppose your son asks for bread. Which of you will give him a stone? . . . You know how to give good gifts to your children. How much more will your Father who is in heaven give good gifts to those who ask him!"

Matthew 7:9, 11

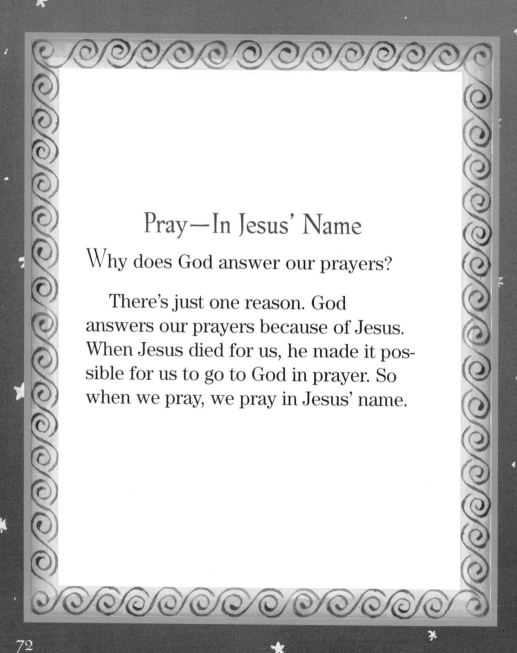

Pray—In Jesus' Name

Why does God answer our prayers?

There's just one reason. God answers our prayers because of Jesus. When Jesus died for us, he made it possible for us to go to God in prayer. So when we pray, we pray in Jesus' name.

A Promise Jesus Made

My Father will give you anything you ask for in my name. Until now you have not asked for anything in my name. Ask, and you will receive what you ask for."

John 16:23–24

God Answers Solomon's Prayer

Read this story in 1 Kings 3:5–13.

When Solomon became king of Israel, God told him, "Ask for anything you want me to give you."

Solomon knew he needed God's help to be king. So he prayed, "Give me a heart that understands. Then I can rule over your people. I can tell the difference between what is right and what is wrong."

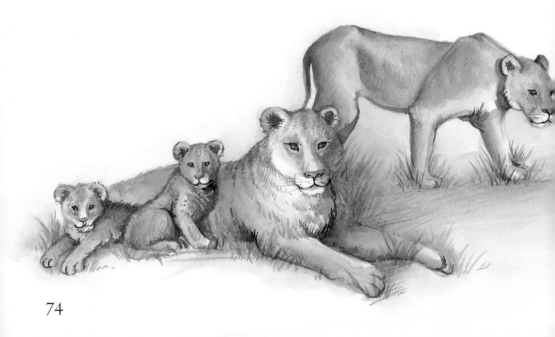

God was pleased with Solomon's prayer. So God said, "I will give you a wise and understanding heart . . . And that is not all. I will give you what you have not asked for. I will give you riches and honor."

Remember:

- God has the power to answer every prayer.
- He can do far more than you ask!

God's Answers

- Sometimes God answers prayer with, "Yes."
- Sometimes God says, "Wait."
- Sometimes God says, "No."

A good parent always says no when children ask to do something that will hurt them, like playing with knives. God is our heavenly parent, so when he says no, it's because he has a good reason and loves us too much to let us have our own way.

God Said No to Jesus

In the Garden of Gethsemane Jesus prayed, "Father, if you are willing, take this cup of suffering away from me. But do what you want, not what I want."

Luke 22:42

God said no to Jesus. God had planned this way to save us. But God did send an angel to strengthen Jesus.

Your Family Prayer Journal

- It's very encouraging to have a notebook in which you can record what your family is praying for.
- Your family can pray for friends, neighbors, teachers, leaders of the country, and missionaries.
- If you leave a space beside each prayer request, you'll be able to record the dates when God answered your family's prayers.

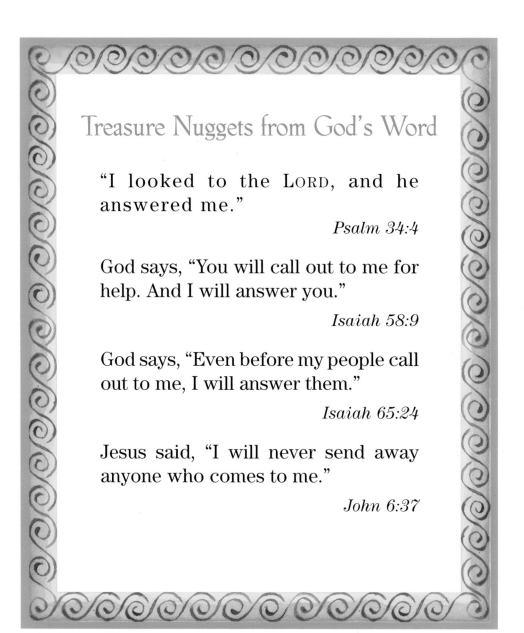

Treasure Nuggets from God's Word

"I looked to the LORD, and he answered me."

Psalm 34:4

God says, "You will call out to me for help. And I will answer you."

Isaiah 58:9

God says, "Even before my people call out to me, I will answer them."

Isaiah 65:24

Jesus said, "I will never send away anyone who comes to me."

John 6:37

II

God Blesses Others
When You Pray

Our prayers are powerful, not because of anything we have done but because God listens when we pray. Think about ways we can help people by praying for them.

Here are some good times to pray:

- When you hear an ambulance.
- When someone is sick.
- When someone gets hurt.

Who does God want you to pray for?

"Pray for everyone. Ask God to bless them. Give thanks for them. Pray for kings. Pray for all who are in authority."

1 Timothy 2:1–2

Pray for Your Enemies

It's easy to love and pray for our friends and people who are nice to us. But it's *not* so easy to love and pray for people who are mean to us.

But when Jesus was whipped and nailed to the cross, he prayed, "Father, forgive them. They don't know what they are doing."

Luke 23:34

Pray for Those Who Hurt You

Jesus said, "You have heard that it was said, 'Love your neighbor. Hate your enemy.' But here is what I tell you. Love your enemies. Pray for those who hurt you. Then you will be sons of your Father who is in heaven."

Matthew 5:43–45

Stop! Think! Pray!

Let's stop and pray for someone who has hurt us.

- Read Jesus' words on page 83 again. Who has been mean to you?
- How could you pray for this person?
- Do you think God can help you forgive this person?
- Will it be easy?
- God will help you and answer your prayer.

Treasure Nuggets from God's Word

Jesus said, "Pray for those who treat you badly."

Luke 6:28

The apostle Paul wrote, "Pray for us too. Pray that God will open a door for our message."

Colossians 4:3

The apostle James wrote "Pray for one another so that you might be healed."

James 5:16

12

God's Angels Guard You

God created everything, from tiny cells to all the stars and planets. God also created an invisible world. Angels are part of this unseen world.

Angels are all around us. If we could see all they do, we would be amazed!

Who Are Angels?

- Angels are spirit beings who are usually invisible.
- Angels do not have parents. God created each angel.
- Angels go where God sends them and do what God tells them.
- Angels praise God.

"Praise the LORD, all you angels in heaven. Praise him, all you who serve him and do what he wants."

Psalm 103:21

Angels Keep You Safe

The LORD says, "I will save the one who loves me. I will keep him safe, because he trusts in me."

Psalm 91:14

One way God keeps us safe is by sending angels to be with us. Angels help us in many ways each day. God wants them to guard everyone who loves and trusts him.

The LORD will command his angels to take good care of you. They will lift you up in their hands. Then you won't trip over a stone."

Psalm 91:11–12

God promises to send angels to help us, watch over us, and care for us. But God did not promise we would *never* get hurt or have an accident. He has promised to be with us no matter what happens.

An Angel in the Lions' Den

God guards the lives of those who are faithful to him" (Psalm 97:10).

When Daniel was in the lions' den, an angel stayed close beside him.

Daniel told the king, "My God sent his angel. And his angel shut the mouths of the lions. They haven't hurt me at all" (Daniel 6:22).

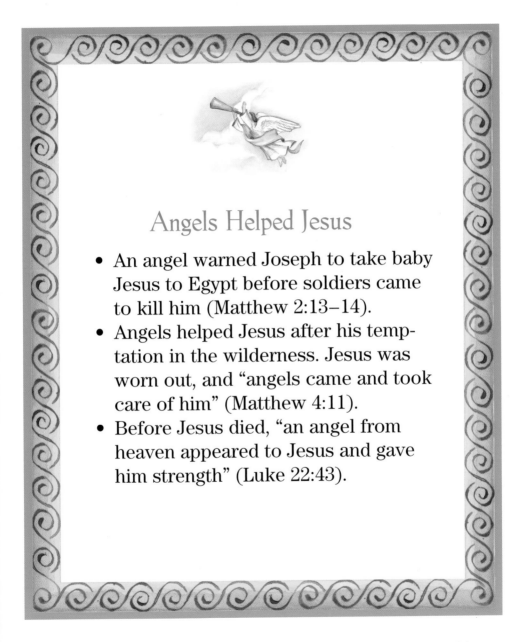

Angels Helped Jesus

- An angel warned Joseph to take baby Jesus to Egypt before soldiers came to kill him (Matthew 2:13–14).
- Angels helped Jesus after his temptation in the wilderness. Jesus was worn out, and "angels came and took care of him" (Matthew 4:11).
- Before Jesus died, "an angel from heaven appeared to Jesus and gave him strength" (Luke 22:43).

Activity Page

- Thank God for his angels, who strengthen and protect us during times of trouble. Make a picture to help you remember angels are watching over you.
- Get out some paper and crayons. Write on the top of your paper, "Angels Watch Over Me." Draw a picture of an angel standing beside you.
- Hang your picture in your bedroom, as a reminder that angels are with you.

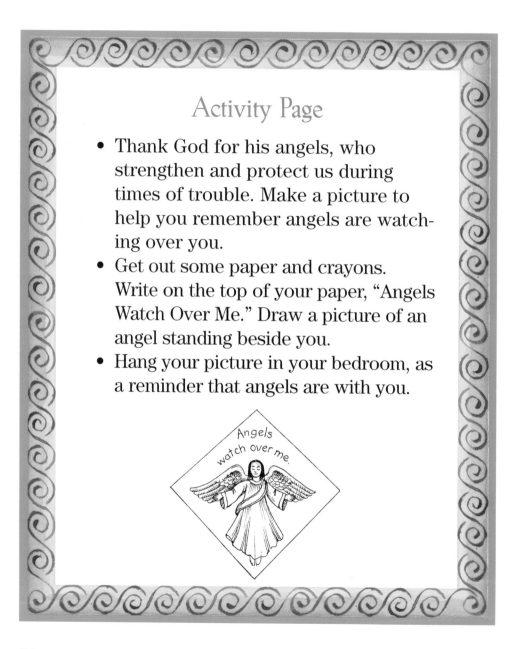

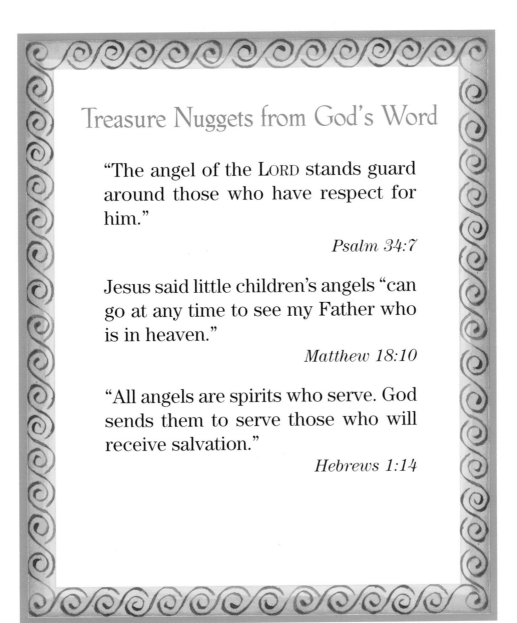

Treasure Nuggets from God's Word

"The angel of the LORD stands guard around those who have respect for him."

Psalm 34:7

Jesus said little children's angels "can go at any time to see my Father who is in heaven."

Matthew 18:10

"All angels are spirits who serve. God sends them to serve those who will receive salvation."

Hebrews 1:14

13

God Helps You During Hard Times

- Problems don't disappear just because we love God.
- In this world we will always have times of pain, sadness, and troubles.
- God has promised to help us during hard times.

"Anyone who does what is right may have many troubles. But the LORD saves him from all of them."

Psalm 34:19

- God promised to be with us through all our troubles.
- No matter what happens, God is there to help us.

We can always say, "The LORD is with me. He helps me."

Psalm 118:7

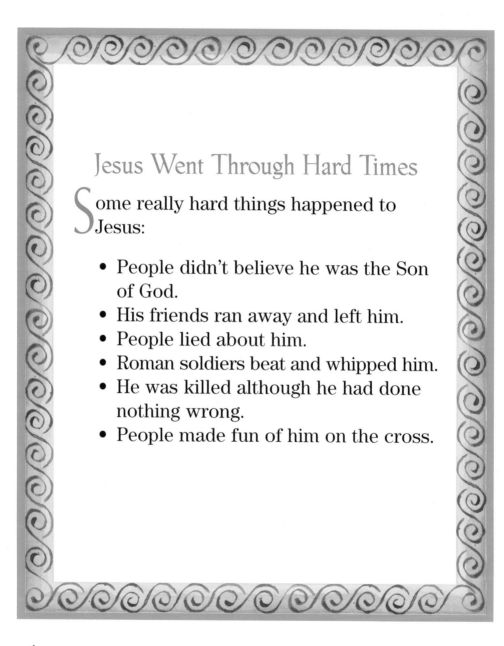

Jesus Went Through Hard Times

Some really hard things happened to Jesus:

- People didn't believe he was the Son of God.
- His friends ran away and left him.
- People lied about him.
- Roman soldiers beat and whipped him.
- He was killed although he had done nothing wrong.
- People made fun of him on the cross.

Jesus never complained or gave up hope. Shortly before he was arrested, he told his friends, "In this world you will have trouble. But cheer up! I have won the battle over the world."

John 16:33

Cheer Up!

How can we be cheerful, even during times of trouble?

It helps to remember:

- Jesus went through greater troubles than we will ever face.
- Jesus was not defeated by those difficulties.
- We are not alone during hard times.
- God will help us.

Here is God's promise to encourage us:

"Do not be afraid ... You belong to me ... I will be with you. You will pass through the rivers. But their waters will not sweep over you. You will walk through fire. But you will not be burned ... I am the LORD your God ... I am the one who saves you."

Isaiah 43:1–3

Activity Page

- Cut out pictures and headlines of disasters from magazines and newspapers.
- Glue them onto a large piece of paper. Pretty awful, isn't it?
- Write one of God's promises from the next page on your paper.
- Hang your paper on the refrigerator, as a reminder that God will help you in every kind of trouble.

My help comes from the Lord.

Treasure Nuggets from God's Word

"God lives forever! You can run to him for safety. His powerful arms are always there to carry you."

Deuteronomy 33:27

"The LORD our God is with us. He will help us."

2 Chronicles 32:8

"God is always there to help us in times of trouble."

Psalm 46:1

"My help comes from the LORD. He is the Maker of heaven and earth."

Psalm 121:2

14

God Gives You Peace

Most people want to live in peace, without fighting or arguing.

But there are things that ruin peace and joy in our homes, schools, neighborhoods, and nations. Some of those things are:

- People who fight and complain.
- Family worries and money problems.
- Kids who act mean and may even be in gangs.
- Violent acts in schools or public places.

When there is no peace around us, we can still be filled with joy and peace because we know God loves us.

God's peace flows through us, calming us and making us happy. God says, "I will cause peace to flow . . . like a river."

Isaiah 66:12

"We have peace with God because of our Lord Jesus Christ."

Romans 5:1

Jesus Gives Peace

Imagine how upset Jesus' disciples felt when he died on the cross. On good Friday they were very sad and distressed about losing their dearest friend. The disciples were also afraid the soldiers might come and arrest them.

On Sunday night, after Jesus rose from the dead, he appeared to his friends and said, "May peace be with you!"

John 20:19

That was good news! The first thing Jesus did was to show them his hands and feet. He made sure they knew he was alive. He even ate some bread while they watched.

Seeing Jesus brought peace into their hearts. Now they knew he was their living Lord and Savior.

Jesus said, "You can have peace because of me."

John 16:33

Peaceful Sleep

Do you ever feel troubled or afraid at bedtime? God especially wants to fill us with peace when we go to bed. We can lie down and sleep in peace. We can trust that God is keeping us safe.

"I will lie down and sleep in peace. LORD, you alone keep me safe."

Psalm 4:8

You can relax and sleep peacefully because

- God sees you even though it's dark.
- God never sleeps.

"The LORD who watches over you won't get tired . . . or go to sleep."

Psalm 121:3–4

LORD, "darkness would not be dark to you. The night would shine like the day, because darkness is like light to you."

Psalm 139:12

Activity Page

- Make a doorhanger by cutting construction paper into a rectangle.
- Trace a circle at the top of the rectangle by drawing around a drinking glass. Cut from the top of the rectangle to the circle.Cut out the circle.
- Print God's promise: "I will lie down and sleep in peace. LORD, you alone keep me safe" (Psalm 4:8).
- Decorate your sign.
- Hang it on your bedroom door to remind you of God's love and care.

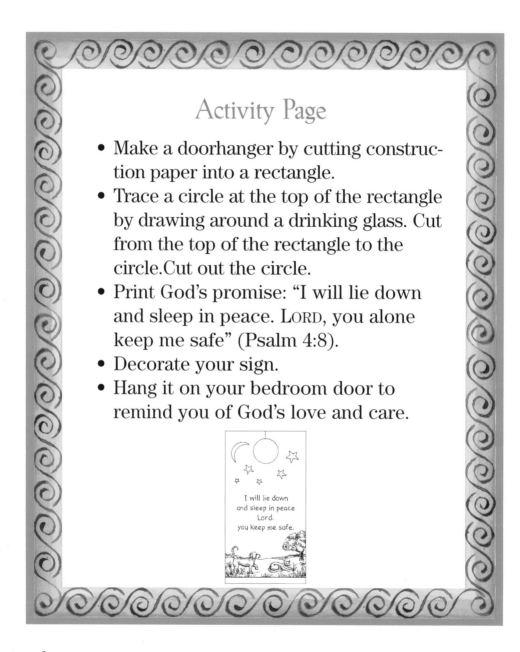

Treasure Nuggets from God's Word

Jesus said, "I give my peace to you. . . .
Do not let your hearts be troubled.
And do not be afraid."

John 14:27

"The God who gives peace will be with
you."

Philippians 4:9

"May the Lord who gives peace give you
peace at all times and in every way."

2 Thessalonians 3:16

15

God Gives You the Holy Spirit

Before he died, Jesus told his friends, "It is for your good that I am going away. Unless I go away, the Holy Spirit will not come to help you. But if I go, I will send him to you."

John 16:7

Who is the Holy Spirit?

- He comes from the heavenly Father.
- He is a Friend sent by Jesus.
- He is part of the Trinity.

What Will the Holy Spirit Do?

Jesus said, "When the Spirit of truth comes, he will guide you into all truth. He will not speak on his own. He will speak only what he hears. And he will tell you what is still going to happen.

He will bring me glory by receiving something from me and showing it to you."

John 16:13–14

Where Is the Holy Spirit?

Jesus promised, "I will ask the Father. And he will give you another Friend to help you and to be with you forever. The Friend is the Spirit of truth . . . The world does not see him or know him. But you know him. He lives with you, and he will be in you."

John 14:16–17

What Is the Holy Spirit's Work?

The Holy Spirit works in us—in our hearts and minds. The Spirit teaches us and reminds us of what Jesus said.

Jesus said, "The Friend is the Holy Sprit. He will teach you all things. He will remind you of everything I have said to you."

John 14:26

Receive God's Gift

Jesus said, "Your Father who is in heaven [will] give the Holy Spirit to those who ask him."

Luke 11:13

If you want to receive this promised gift:

- Ask God to give you the Holy Spirit.
- Thank God for the gift of his Spirit.
- Trust that God has given you his Spirit if you have asked.

Treasure Nuggets from God's Word

In the last days, God says, "I will pour out my Spirit on all people."

Joel 2:28

Jesus said, "John baptized with water. But ... you will be baptized with the Holy Spirit."

Acts 1:5

"Because you are his children, God sent the Spirit of his Son into our hearts."

Galatians 4:6

16

God Guides Us

When we were babies, we couldn't make any choices. But as we grew older, we learned to think about what we would or wouldn't do.

God has given us the ability to make decisions. He will always guide us in our choices.

The LORD promises, "I will always guide you."

Isaiah 58:11

You can ask God for help in making decisions.

"If any of you need wisdom, ask God for it. He will give it to you."

James 1:5

- What decisions must you make now?
- Is your family making plans?

This is a good time to pray. God's job is to guide us. Our job is to ask for his guidance.

God Guides Butterflies

Each year millions of Eastern Monarch butterflies hatch out of cocoons all over the United States. In the fall they fly south to Mexico.

They all arrive at the same grove of trees about the same time! This is amazing because none of them has ever been there before.

How do they find their way? Only God knows.

In the spring the butterflies turn around and fly north to lay eggs. Soon their children will make the amazing journey to Mexico!

What About Us?

If God leads small butterflies to a safe place for the winter, we can trust him to lead us every day.

God will help us know what to do and where to go. All we have to do is trust his promises.

"I will guide you and teach you the way you should go."

Psalm 32:8

Activity Page

- Make a butterfly collage. Draw an outline of a large butterfly on a piece of white paper. Look at the picture on this page.
- Cut construction paper of many colors into small triangles and squares.
- Glue these pieces all over the wings of the butterfly.
- Ask an adult to help you cut out the butterfly.
- Tape it on your front door to remind you that God leads you.

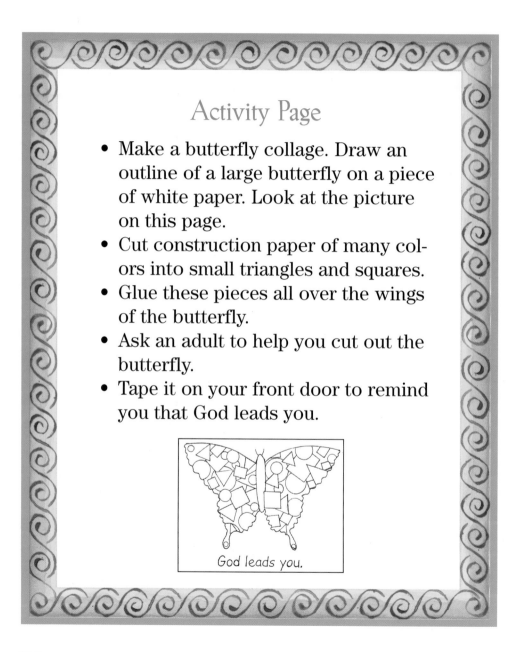

God leads you.

Treasure Nuggets from God's Word

"The LORD is my shepherd ... He leads me."

Psalm 23:1–2

"I will guide you."

Psalm 32:8

"I am the LORD your God. I teach you what is best for you. I direct you in the way you should go."

Isaiah 48:17

"The LORD will go ahead of you and lead you."

Isaiah 52:12

17

God Gives You Strength

We all have times when we're afraid. But God wants us to be strong and brave as we trust him.

God often says in the Bible, "Do not be afraid."

Long ago God told his people, "Be strong, all of you people in the land … I am with you … So do not be afraid."

Haggai 2:4–5

During difficult and fearful times, we can rely on God's promises.

- God wants to strengthen us.
- God doesn't want us to be afraid of what will happen.
- Trusting God will help us be strong and brave when we face the future.

A Strong Shield

Long ago it was very important to have a sturdy shield—a shield could save your life. Shields were several feet wide and were made of strong wood or metal. A shield was good protection from spears, swords, and flying arrows.

God told Abram, "Do not be afraid. I am like a shield to you."

Genesis 15:1

God is our shield.

"God is my loving God . . . He is like a shield that keeps me safe. I go to him for safety."

Psalm 144:2

Activity Page

- Draw a shield on a piece of cardboard.
- Ask an adult to cut it out.
- Decorate your shield.
- Tape a strip of cardboard on the back of the shield for a handle.
- On your shield write God's promise:

"The LORD gives me strength. He is like a shield that keeps me safe."

Psalm 28:7

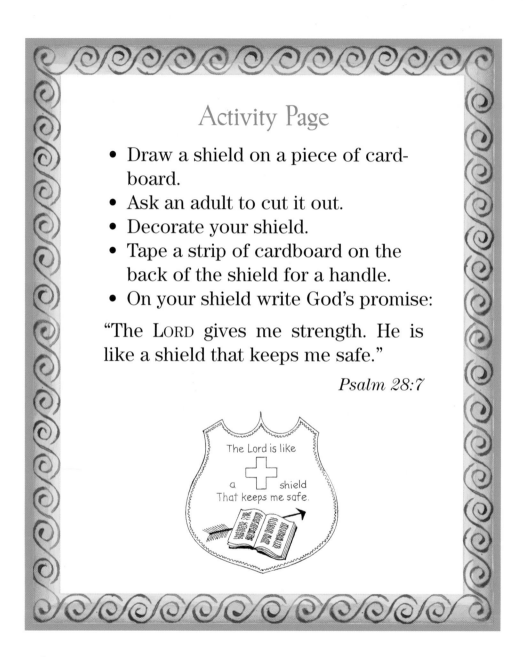

Treasure Nuggets from God's Word

"Those who trust in the LORD will receive new strength."

Isaiah 40:31

The LORD says, "Do not be afraid. I am with you.... I will make you strong and help you."

Isaiah 41:10

"God will keep you strong to the very end."

1 Corinthians 1:8

"Depend on God's mighty power."

Ephesians 6:10

18

God Works Everything for Good

Even when everything goes wrong, we can be sure of two things:

- God loves us and is with us.
- God promised to bring good out of everything—even bad things like accidents, sickness, and death.

"We know that in all things God works for the good of those who love him."

Romans 8:28

What Will We Do When Things Go Wrong?

- Will we blame God for our troubles?
- Will we feel angry with God if we have an accident?
- Will we wonder if God loves us when bad things happen?
- Or will we trust God to work everything out for our good—no matter what happens?

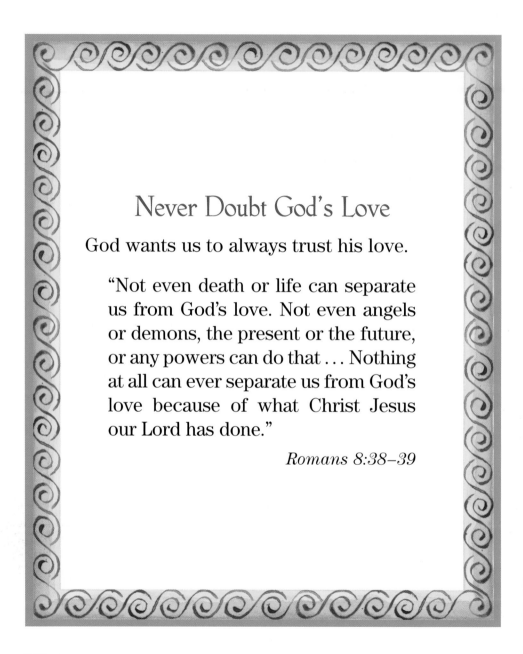

Never Doubt God's Love

God wants us to always trust his love.

"Not even death or life can separate us from God's love. Not even angels or demons, the present or the future, or any powers can do that ... Nothing at all can ever separate us from God's love because of what Christ Jesus our Lord has done."

Romans 8:38–39

Struggles Strengthen Us

A butterfly breaking out of its cocoon must work hard to free itself. But the struggle makes blood flow out to the tips of the butterfly's wings. That helps the wings become strong. Without the struggle, the butterfly's wings will be useless. And the butterfly will never fly—it will only grow weak and finally die!

Joseph's Troubles

Remember Joseph from the Old Testament?

- His jealous brothers threw him into a pit (Genesis 37:2–24).
- They sold him to slave traders (Genesis 37:25–28).
- The slave traders sold him to Potiphar (Genesis 37:36).
- Potiphar's wife lied about Joseph (Genesis 39:1–19).
- Potiphar put Joseph in prison because of the lie (Genesis 39:20–23).

After that Pharaoh had strange dreams. He learned Joseph could explain them. So he sent for Joseph.

God helped Joseph explain the dreams. Pharaoh put Joseph in charge of storing grain. When a famine came, there was plenty of food (Genesis 41:1–49, 53–57).

Later Joseph told his brothers, "You planned to harm me. But God planned it for good" (Genesis 50:20).

Activity Page

- To make a Bible book mark use construction paper to make a Bible bookmark and cut out a rectangle two inches wide by six inches long.
- Read, and if you can, memorize Romans 8:28 (on the next page.)
- Write, "Romans 8:28" and "God is good! God works all for good!" on your bookmark.
- Draw leaves or flowers to decorate your bookmark. Seal it with clear contact paper.

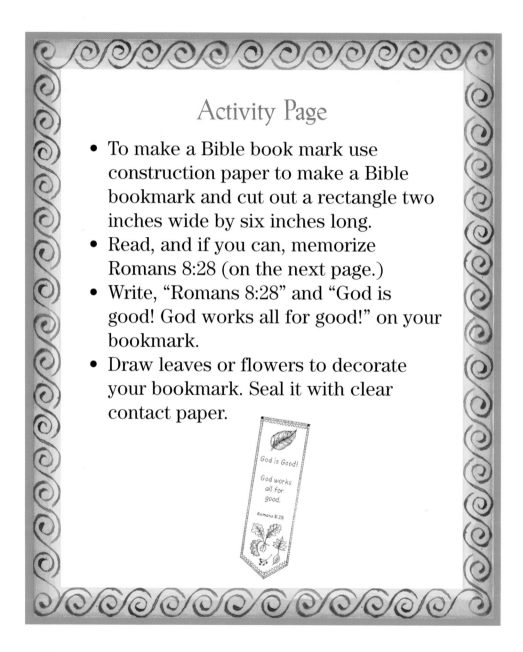

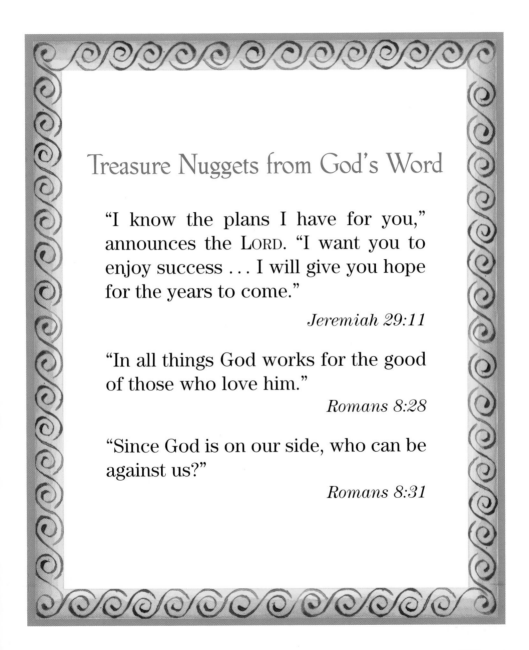

Treasure Nuggets from God's Word

"I know the plans I have for you," announces the LORD. "I want you to enjoy success ... I will give you hope for the years to come."

Jeremiah 29:11

"In all things God works for the good of those who love him."

Romans 8:28

"Since God is on our side, who can be against us?"

Romans 8:31

God Blesses All
Who Give

Jesus promised, "Give, and it will be given to you. A good amount will be poured into your lap. It will be pressed down, shaken together, and running over. The same amount you give will be measured out to you."

Luke 6:38

We can choose to be generous. Or we can choose to be selfish. God wants us to be generous and then he will give generously to us. We have to decide. Will we be generous—or stingy?

Jesus said, "You have received freely, so give freely."

Matthew 10:8

Share Your Riches

Jesus said, "Use the riches of this world to help others. In that way, you will make friends for yourselves. Then when your riches are gone, you will be welcomed into your eternal home in heaven."

Luke 16:9

God has given us many gifts. But these are not just for our enjoyment. God wants us to share them.

To Whom Will You Give?

- Has anyone asked you for something lately?
- Has anyone wanted to borrow something?
- What did you do when that person asked?

Jesus said, "Give to the one who asks you for something. Don't turn away from the one who wants to borrow something from you."

Matthew 5:42

Be a Secret Giver

Jesus said, "When you give to the needy, don't let your left hand know what your right hand is doing. Then your giving will be done secretly. Your Father will reward you. He sees what you do secretly."

Matthew 6:3–4

- What secret giving could you do today?
- When have you given something secretly?

Give—to Your Enemies!

- It is easy to do good to those who love us.
- We also need to do good to those who hurt us.

Jesus said, "Love your enemies. Do good to them. Lend to them without expecting to get anything back. Then you will receive a lot in return."

Luke 6:35

Activity Page

- Who in your neighborhood needs a gift? An elderly person, someone not well liked, a bully?
- What could you give? Freshly baked cookies, homemade rolls, a plant or a bouquet of flowers, a card?
- Prepare your gift. Pray for the person before you deliver it.
- It's fun to give your gift secretly!

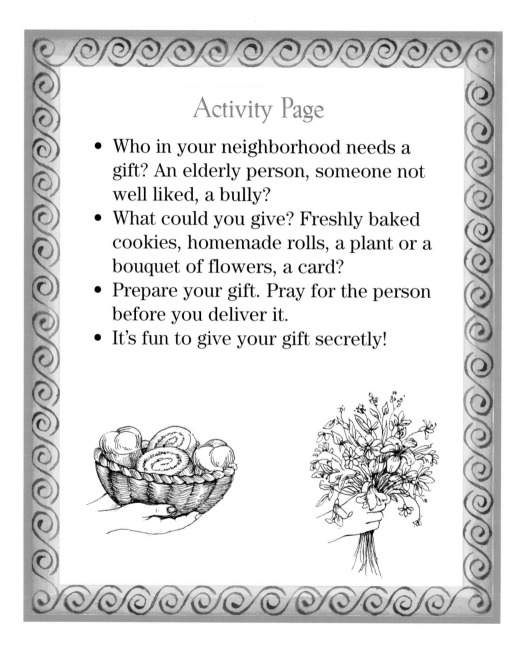

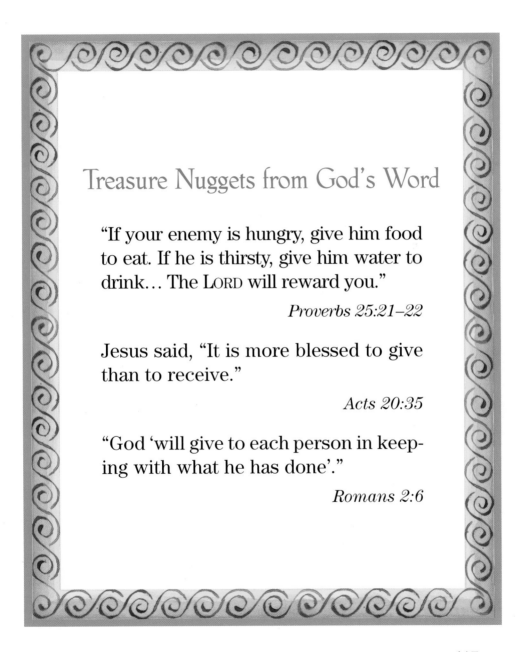

Treasure Nuggets from God's Word

"If your enemy is hungry, give him food to eat. If he is thirsty, give him water to drink… The LORD will reward you."

Proverbs 25:21–22

Jesus said, "It is more blessed to give than to receive."

Acts 20:35

"God 'will give to each person in keeping with what he has done'."

Romans 2:6

20

God Cares for the Poor

- God cares about poor people.
- God wants us to care about them, too.
- A great reward is promised if we help those who have nothing.

"Anyone who is kind to poor people lends to the LORD. God will reward him for what he has done."

Proverbs 19:17

God promises to bless all our work, and everything we do when we give to those in need.

"Give freely to those who are needy. Open your hearts to them. Then the LORD your God will bless you in all of your work. He will bless you in everything you do."

Deuteronomy 15:10

Who Will You Invite?

It's easy to give to loved ones. But Jesus wants us to share with many other people, too.

Jesus said, "Suppose you give a lunch or a dinner … Do not invite your friends, your brothers or sisters, or your relatives, or your rich neighbors. If you do, they may invite you to eat with them. So you will be paid back."

Luke 14:12

Jesus continued, "But when you give a big dinner, invite those who are poor. Also invite those who can't walk, the disabled and the blind. Then you will be blessed. Your guests can't pay you back. But you will be paid back when those who are right with God rise from the dead."

Luke 14:13–14

Activity Page

- Cover a shoebox with wrapping paper. Wrap the lid separately.
- Decide who will get the box. A poor family, a homeless shelter, missionaries?
- Fill the box with wrapped candy, stickers, pens, markers, notepads, toothbrushes, washcloths, small balls, toys.
- Make and sign a card for whoever will receive the box.
- Pray for them.

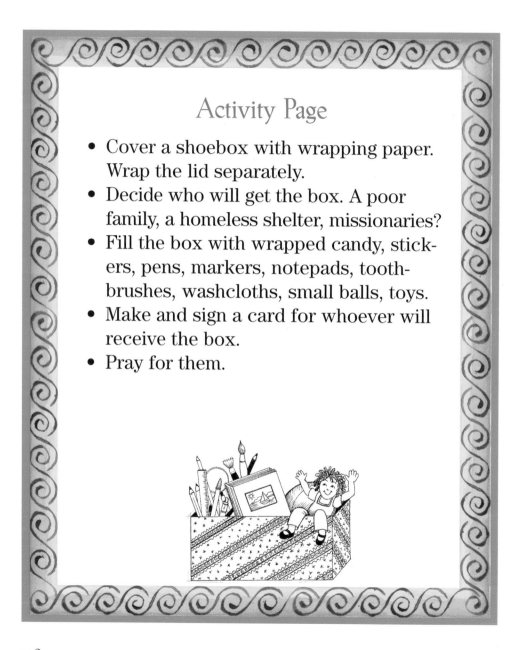

Treasure Nuggets from God's Word

"Blessed is the person who is kind to those in need."

Proverbs 14:21

"Anyone who gives freely will be blessed. That's because he shares his food with those who are poor."

Proverbs 22:9

Jesus said, "When you give to the needy . . . your Father will reward you. He sees what you do secretly."

Matthew 6:3–4

21

Jesus Promised to Come Again

The night before Jesus was crucified, his disciples became upset when he told them he would be leaving soon.

Jesus said, "Do not let your hearts be troubled. Trust in God. Trust in me also ... I am going ... to prepare a place for you ... I will come back. And I will take you to be with me."

John 14:1–3

Forty days after Jesus rose from the dead, he blessed his disciples. Then he went up into the sky and disappeared into a cloud.

Two men dressed in white appeared and asked, "Why do you stand here looking at the sky? Jesus has been taken away from you into heaven. But he will come back in the same way you saw him go."

Acts 1:11

When Will He Return?

Even though we know for sure that Jesus will
come back to earth, no one knows exactly
when it will happen.

Jesus said, "No one knows about that day or
hour. Not even the angels in heaven know. The
Son does not know. Only the Father knows."

Matthew 24:36.

What Will Happen?

Read 1 Thessalonians 4:16–17.

- Jesus will come down from heaven.
- We will hear a loud command.
- We will hear the voice of the angels' leader.
- We will hear a blast from God's trumpet.
- We will be taken up into the clouds.
- We will meet Jesus in the air.
- We will be with Jesus forever.

All the nations on earth ... will see Jesus coming on the clouds of the sky. He will come with power and great glory. He will send his angels with a loud trumpet call. They will gather his chosen people from all four directions."

Matthew 24:30–31

Won't you be excited when you get to meet Jesus in the sky?

Plants and Birds Come Back

You can be sure that tulips will come up again each spring. You can bet that birds who fly south for the winter will return.

We can also trust Jesus to keep his promise to return.

Jesus promised, "I will come back. And I will take you to be with me."

John 14:3

Activity Page

- To make a victory pennant, get out construction paper, scissors, and markers.
- Cut the paper into a triangle-shaped pennant.
- Use markers to write this promise on your pennant: Jesus said, "I am coming soon" (Revelation 3:11).
- Attach colorful ribbons to the wide end of the pennant.
- Hang up the pennant as a reminder of Jesus' return.

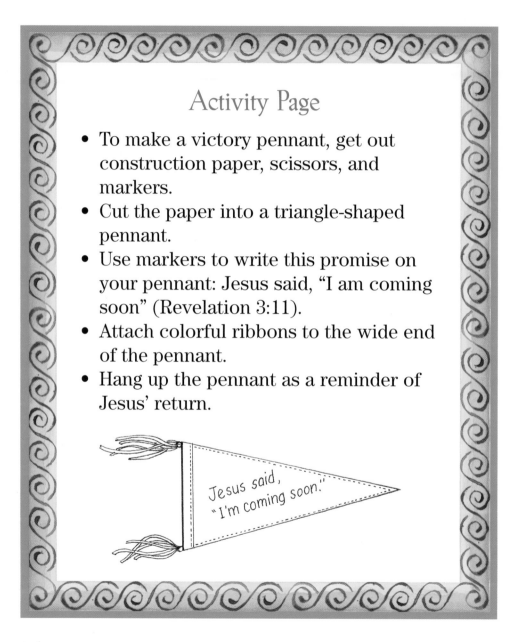

Jesus said, "I'm coming soon."

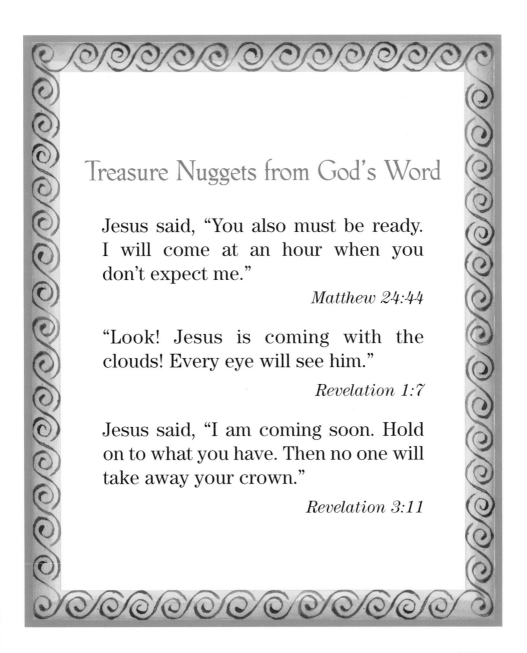

Treasure Nuggets from God's Word

Jesus said, "You also must be ready. I will come at an hour when you don't expect me."

Matthew 24:44

"Look! Jesus is coming with the clouds! Every eye will see him."

Revelation 1:7

Jesus said, "I am coming soon. Hold on to what you have. Then no one will take away your crown."

Revelation 3:11

22

God Will Give You a New Body

Everyone who is born will die some-day. But we don't have to be afraid of death. God has given us some wonderful promises:

- Our lives do not end when we die.
- God has a new and wonderful life waiting for us in heaven.
- God will give us new bodies.

God raised Jesus from the dead. Now Jesus gives us the promise of eternal life.

Aren't you glad to know we will live even if we die?

Jesus said, "I am the resurrection and the life. Anyone who believes in me will live, even if he dies. And those who live and believe in me will never die."

John 11:25–26

Jesus was the first person raised from the dead, never to die again. And Jesus promised, "Because I live, you will live also."

John 14:19

"Christ is the first of those who rise from the dead. When he comes back, those who belong to him will be raised. Then the end will come."

1 Corinthians 15:23–24

A New Body

God promises to change our human bodies of flesh and blood into bodies that will never die.

It won't take long—our bodies will be changed in a *flash* when Jesus returns to earth.

- Our bodies will be powerful.
- Our bodies will glorious.
- Our bodies will be strong.
- Our bodies will not hurt.

What Will Our New Bodies Look Like?

J esus will change our earthly bodies. They will become like his glorious body."

Philippians 3:21

"We know that when Christ appears, we will be like him. We will see him as he really is."

1 John 3:2

Just Like Jesus

Our bodies will be like Jesus' body after he rose from the dead. Let's see what kind of body that was.

- Jesus still looked like himself.
- He could appear and disappear without using doors.
- Jesus' body could be touched but could no longer be injured.
- Jesus' body had scars, but they didn't hurt.

Activity Page

- Make a picture by laying a piece of paper lengthwise. Write, "New Bodies" on top.
- On the left side of the paper draw a caterpillar.
- Draw a cocoon in the middle.
- On the right side draw a beautiful butterfly!
- Tape this picture above your bed, as a reminder that God promises you a new, heavenly body.

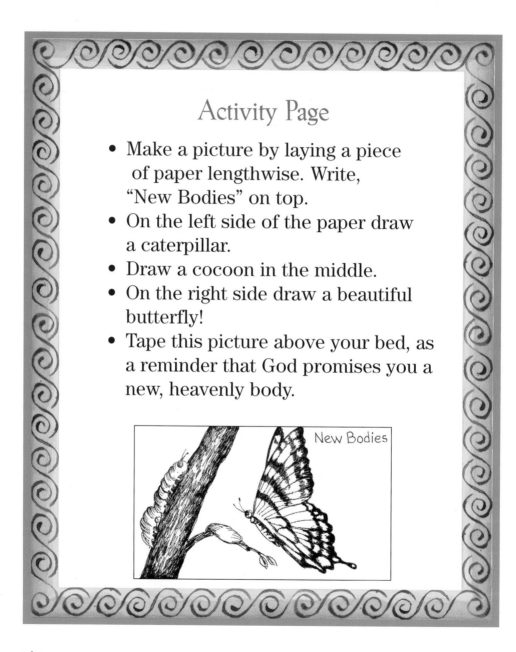

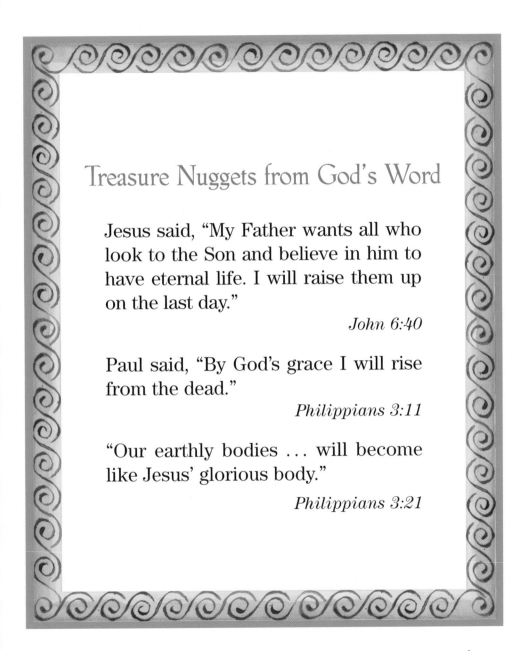

Treasure Nuggets from God's Word

Jesus said, "My Father wants all who look to the Son and believe in him to have eternal life. I will raise them up on the last day."

John 6:40

Paul said, "By God's grace I will rise from the dead."

Philippians 3:11

"Our earthly bodies ... will become like Jesus' glorious body."

Philippians 3:21

23

God Will Give You a Home in Heaven

God loves us so much that he wants us to live with him forever. God offers us a wonderful home in heaven!

"God loved the world so much that he gave his one and only Son. Anyone who believes in him will not die but will have eternal life."

John 3:16

Who Gets a Home in Heaven?

- No one gets to heaven by doing good deeds.
- Heaven is our home because of what Jesus has done.
- When we receive Jesus as our Savior, we can be sure we will live forever in heaven.

"God gives you the gift of eternal life because of what Christ Jesus our Lord has done."

Romans 6:23

God wants you to be happy as you look forward to living with him.

- Jesus said, "Be glad that your names are written in heaven."

Luke 10:20

- "God will bring you into his heavenly glory . . . with great joy."

Jude 24

Aren't you happy that your name is written in God's Book of Life?

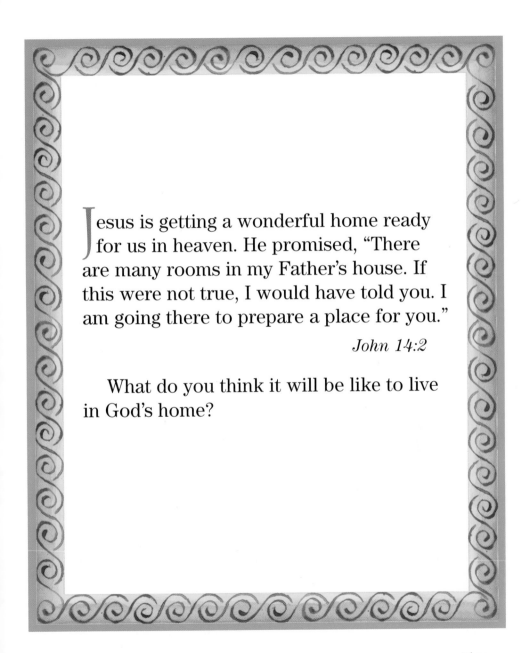

Jesus is getting a wonderful home ready for us in heaven. He promised, "There are many rooms in my Father's house. If this were not true, I would have told you. I am going there to prepare a place for you."

John 14:2

What do you think it will be like to live in God's home?

No More Tears

There will always be tears and sadness here on this earth. But whenever we feel sad, we need to stop and remember what life in heaven will be like someday.

"God will wipe away every tear ... There will no be more death or sadness. There will be no more crying or pain."

Revelation 21:4

God's Promise of Heaven

God's servants will serve him. They will see his face. His name will be on their foreheads.

There will be no more night. They will not need the light of a lamp or the light of the sun. The Lord God will give them light. They will rule for ever and ever."

Revelation 22:3–5

Animal Homes

God gave the animals special abilities to make wonderful homes for their babies.

- Beavers cut down trees to build homes in the water.
- Wolves dig tunnels that lead to underground dens.
- Polar bears hollow out dens in the snowdrifts. They often make extra spaces as playrooms for their cubs.

If polar bears and wolves and beavers know exactly what their babies need, how much more does God know how to make the perfect home for you in heaven?

Jesus is preparing some special surprises in heaven. You can be sure he knows what will make you very, very happy!

Activity Page

- Make a heaven mobile by cutting from construction paper a circle, a house, a crown, and a cloud.
- Write, "I will live" on the circle, "in the house" on the house, "of the LORD" on the crown, and "forever" on the cloud (Psalm 23:6).
- Tie the shapes to a clothes hanger.
- Hang your mobile up as a reminder of your home in heaven.

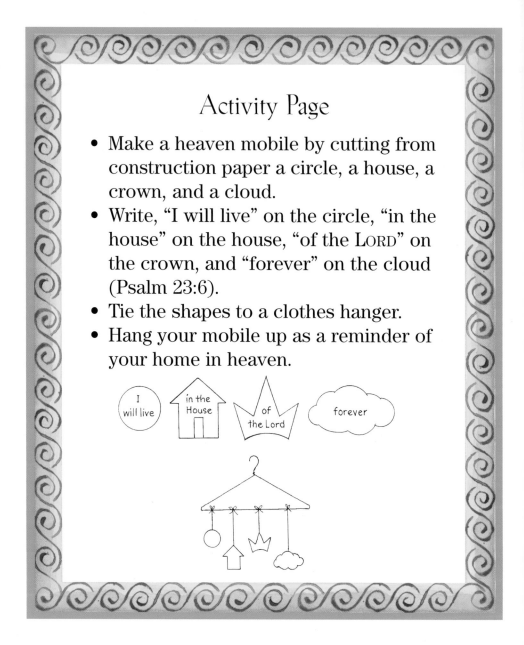

Treasure Nuggets from God's Word

"I will live in the house of the LORD forever."

Psalm 23:6

"The Lord ... will bring me safely to his heavenly kingdom."

2 Timothy 4:18

"God has given us eternal life. That life is found in his Son. Those who belong to the Son have life."

1 John 5:11–12

24

God Will Reward
Every Good Deed

Good deeds will never get anyone into heaven. Jesus is the only way to heaven.

Jesus said, "I am the way and the truth and the life. No one comes to the Father except through me."

John 14:6

But God still wants us to do good deeds. He promises a reward for all we do.

Jesus said, "Look! I am coming soon! I bring my rewards with me. I will reward each person for what he has done."

Revelation 22:12

Rewards

What do you think God might give us as rewards?

- God will give greater rewards than anyone can imagine.
- God promised to reward us and we can trust his promises.
- God will have some fun, creative, and interesting rewards waiting for us in heaven!

Whom Do You Serve?

What work did you do this week? Did you do it well?

"Work at everything you do with all your heart. Work as if you were working for the Lord, not for human masters. Work because you know that you will finally receive as a reward what the Lord wants you to have. You are serving the Lord Christ."

Colossians 3:23–24

Activity Page

- Cut out two paper hearts.
- Decorate both hearts and tape them together to form a pocket.
- Cut strips of paper to make coupons.
- Write some tasks you will do this week for others.
- Fold the coupons and stuff them into your heart container. Let others pull out a coupon. Serve them as the coupon says.

God rewards every good deed.

I will clean my room.

I will take the garbage out

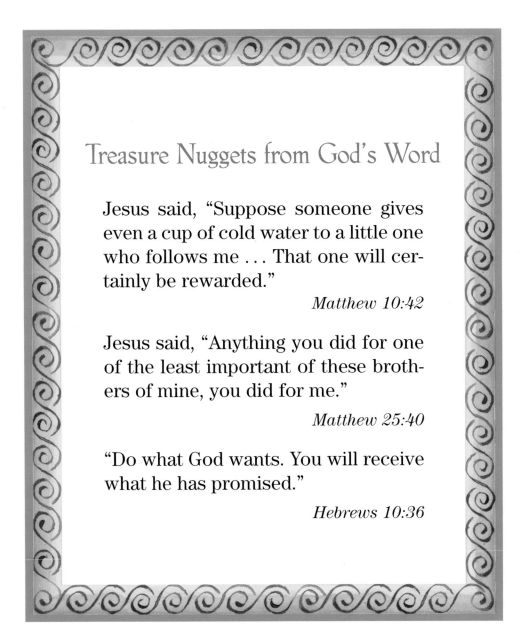

Treasure Nuggets from God's Word

Jesus said, "Suppose someone gives even a cup of cold water to a little one who follows me ... That one will certainly be rewarded."

Matthew 10:42

Jesus said, "Anything you did for one of the least important of these brothers of mine, you did for me."

Matthew 25:40

"Do what God wants. You will receive what he has promised."

Hebrews 10:36

25

God Will Never Leave You

Though we cannot see God, we can be sure God is with us and will never leave us.

"God is always there to help us."

Psalm 46:1

Just before Jesus went up into heaven, he gave his friends this promise: "You can be sure that I am always with you, to the very end."

Matthew 28:20

Jesus promised to stay close to us. In fact, he said he would make his *home* with us when we love him and obey his teaching.

Jesus said, "Anyone who loves me will obey my teaching. My Father will love him. We will come to him and make our home with him."

John 14:23

Stay Close to Jesus!

We are like branches on a vine. If a branch breaks off, it dries up and dies.

Jesus is the vine. We stay connected to him through praying and reading the Bible.

Jesus said, "If anyone remains joined to me, and I to him, he will bear a lot of fruit. You can't do anything without me."

John 15:5

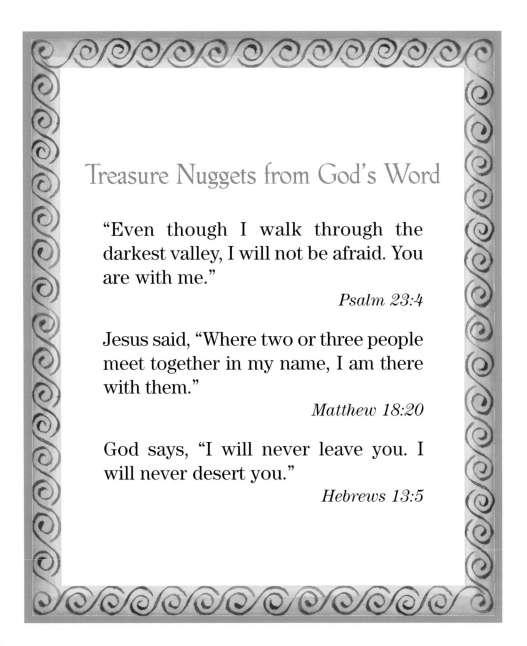

Treasure Nuggets from God's Word

"Even though I walk through the darkest valley, I will not be afraid. You are with me."

Psalm 23:4

Jesus said, "Where two or three people meet together in my name, I am there with them."

Matthew 18:20

God says, "I will never leave you. I will never desert you."

Hebrews 13:5

26

God Will Honor Your Faith

God has given us many promises. Now what will *you* do? Will you trust his promises?

Remember,
- God said, "I am the LORD... Is anything too hard for me?"
  Jeremiah 32:27

- "Nothing is impossible with God."
  Luke 1:37

- "God is able to do far more than we could ever ask for or imagine."
  Ephesians 3:20

Seed Faith

Jesus said, "If you have faith as small as a mustard seed, ... you can say to this mountain, 'Move from here to there.' And it will move. Nothing will be impossible for you."

Matthew 17:20–21

- A mustard seed is tiny but grows into a big bush.
- Faith, like a seed, must always be growing.
- Nothing is impossible when we trust God.

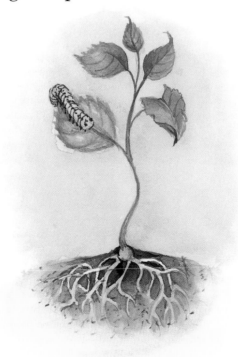

Keep on Believing!

A mother kept following Jesus. She wouldn't leave until Jesus healed her daughter. Jesus told her, "You have great faith! You will be given what you are asking for."

Matthew 15:28

Ask yourself:

- Will we trust Jesus' promises?
- Will God honor our faith and give us all he has promised?

Believe:

- God, together with us, make a great team!

Treasure Nuggets from God's Word

"The LORD your God is God. He is the faithful God. He keeps his [promises] … with those who love him and obey his commands. He shows them his love."

Deuteronomy 7:9

"We live by believing, not by seeing."

2 Corinthians 5:7

"Someday we will receive all that God has promised."

Ephesians 1:14

27

Your Gift to God

This book is full of the great promises of God.

God has given so much to us.

Now let's talk about what we can give back to God. You can thank God and say,

"I accept your promises.

I trust that you will do what you say.

Now I give you my life."

Commit your life to the LORD. Here is what he will do if you trust in him. He will make your godly ways shine like the dawn. He will make your honest life shine like the sun at noon."

Psalm 37:5–6

With God's help you will love, serve, pray, share, forgive, and be faithful and strong.

God will make you shine like the sun!

We want to hear from you. Please send your comments about this
book to us in care of the address below. Thank you.

Zonder**kidz**™

Grand Rapids, MI 49530
www.zonderkidz.com